Adventures of Riley

Riddle of the Reef

Adventures of Riley®
Riddle of the Reef

Dear Riley,

Australia's Great Barrier Reef is in great danger! Large areas of the reef, which is made of coral, are dying. We need to find out why!

Aunt Martha, Cousin Alice, and I are flying to Australia to see what's up Down Under, and we want you to come along. Can you help us solve this reef riddle?

Uncle Max

BY
Amanda Lumry
AND
Laura Hurwitz

SCHOLASTIC INC.

New York • Toronto • London • Auckland • Sydney
Mexico City • New Delhi • Hong Kong • Buenos Aires

A special thank-you to all the scientists who collaborated on this project. Your time and assistance are very much appreciated.

www.eaglemont.com

All photographs by Amanda Lumry except:
Cover coral island and page 2 Brisbane skyline © Jeremy Woodhouse/ Getty Images
Endpapers reef © John W. Banagan/Getty Images
Pages 4–5 reef © Stephen Frink/Getty Images
Page 10 blue tang © DEA/C DANI/Getty Images
Pages 10–11 coral reef fauna and page 28 coral reef © Jeff Hunter/ Getty Images
Page 12 water surface © Oliver Strewe/Getty Images
Page 13 underwater coral © Stuart Westmorland/Getty Images
Page 20 lionfish © Don Farrall/Getty Images
Page 21 dugong and pages 22–23 great white shark © Mike Parry/Getty Images
Pages 24–25 aerial island © Annie Griffiths Belt/Getty Images

Illustrations and Layouts by Ulkutay & Ulkutay, London WC2E 9RZ
Editing and Digital Compositing by Michael E. Penman
Digital Imaging by Quebecor World Premedia

ISBN-13: 978-0-545-06848-2
ISBN-10: 0-545-06848-7

10 9 8 7 6 5 4 3 2 1   09 10 11 12 13

Printed in the U.S.A.   08
First Scholastic paperback printing, February 2009

FSC
Mixed Sources
Product group from well-managed forests, controlled sources and recycled wood or fiber
Cert no. SGS-COC-003338
www.fsc.org
© 1996 Forest Stewardship Council

A portion of the proceeds from your purchase of this licensed product supports the stated educational mission of the Smithsonian Institution— "the increase and diffusion of knowledge." The name of the Smithsonian Institution and the sunburst logo are registered trademarks of the Smithsonian Institution and are registered in the U.S. Patent and Trademark Office. www.si.edu

2% of the proceeds from this book will be donated to the Wildlife Conservation Society. http://wcs.org

We try to produce the most beautiful books possible and we are extremely concerned about the impact of our manufacturing process on the forests of the world and the environment as a whole. Accordingly, we made sure that the paper used in this book has been certified as coming from forests that are managed to ensure the protection of the people and wildlife dependent upon them.

"Mom! Our water is brown!"
said Riley.

"The storm has washed a lot of **sediment** into the water system," said his mother. "Until the water clears up, we can't take showers, wash the dishes, or even make juice! At least you'll have clean water in Australia."

Riley flew to Los Angeles, where he caught a flight to eastern Australia.
He landed in Brisbane, which is near the Great Barrier Reef.

Uncle Max, Aunt Martha, and Cousin Alice met Riley at the airport.

"G'day, mate! We have to keep moving so we don't miss our flight north to Gladstone," said Aunt Martha.

"From there we'll take a helicopter to Heron Island, where our research boat is waiting," said Uncle Max.

Coral

A coral reef produces its own sunscreen, using the same chemical in the sunscreen that humans use.

▶ Corals are like tiny anemones or jellyfish. Over 3 million little algae live in their skin and produce energy for them to feed on.

▶ The Great Barrier Reef is so large, it can be seen from outer space!

—Tim McClanahan, Ph.D.,
Senior Conservation Zoologist,
Wildlife Conservation Society

On the flight to Heron Island, Riley caught his first glimpse of the Great Barrier Reef.

"Wow! It goes on forever!" said Riley.

"It's the largest coral reef system in the world," said Aunt Martha. "And it provides shelter and food for thousands of plant and animal species."

"Did you know that the reef is made up of billions of coral **polyps**, which are living animals?" said Uncle Max. "Coral starts out as a tiny **larva**, which attaches to the reef or another hard surface, then grows into a **polyp** about the size of a pencil eraser. The **polyp** then builds a hard calcium skeleton, and over time divides into more **polyps**, forming a coral colony. These skeletons form the reef and remain even after the coral dies."

5

Coral Life Cycle

1. Coral eggs are released.

2. The eggs develop into **larvae**.

3. The **larvae** drift until they find a safe spot to stick to.

4. The **larvae** grow **tentacles** and become coral **polyps**.

5. The **polyps** grow hard skeletons and divide into other **polyps**.

6. After one year, the new **polyp** colony is ready to release eggs.

6

After landing, Uncle Max pointed to a large boat tied up to the dock. "Here's our floating lab," he said.

"Max!" said a man on the deck.

"Wyland, my friend!" said Uncle Max. "Alice and Riley, meet Wyland. His sea-life murals have made him famous, and his love of the oceans has made him an expert on water conservation. I'm thrilled he could join our mission!"

"I wouldn't miss it!" said Wyland. "I was already in Australia getting ideas for my next mural. Plus, I'll do whatever it takes to help save the reef from bleaching."

7

"My mom bleaches my uniform after soccer practice. Is that what you mean?" asked Riley.

"Not quite," said Uncle Max. Riley blushed.

"No need to be embarrassed, Riley. That was a great question," Uncle Max said. "While bleaching makes white clothes look bright and new, for coral, turning white is a bad thing."

"I still don't understand," said Riley.

Sunken Ship,
HMCS *Protector*

8

Uncle Max continued. "When ocean temperatures rise, or when water quality turns bad, the tiny **algae** that provide nutrients and color to coral will leave. This causes the coral to turn white. If water conditions don't improve soon enough, the **algae** won't come back. The coral will then starve and die. Without living coral, the reef, and the reef ecosystem, will collapse and never recover."

"Now I get it," said Riley.

For their first dive, they placed special sensors along a healthy reef to check water temperatures. The reef looked like a giant aquarium full of brightly colored fish and coral. It was easy to see why it is called the rain forest of the sea!

Octopus

➤ It can quickly change its skin color and texture to match its surroundings. This makes it very hard to spot!

➤ A female may lay up to 600,000 eggs at a time!

—Ellen E. Strong, Ph.D., Curator of Mollusks, Department of Invertebrate Zoology, National Museum of Natural History, Smithsonian Institution

"Hey Riley, can you help me with this sensor?" asked Wyland. "Remember not to touch the coral."

"Why?" asked Riley. "I thought coral was hard."

"The skeletons are hard, but the **polyps** inside stay soft," said Wyland. "Even the slightest touch can harm them."

"Okay," said Riley.

Riley dove underwater to place the sensor, and found himself face-to-face with a giant starfish. Aunt Martha wrote DANGER on her wrist slate and showed Riley.

"Those are crown-of-thorns starfish," said Aunt Martha after they surfaced. "They prey on coral and their spines have venom in them. If you get pricked by one, it would really hurt!" They got back in the boat and headed north to study an area that had been bleached for a long time.

DANGER

Crown-of-Thorns Starfish

➤ It has five arms when it is young but grows up to 20 arms as an adult. Each arm is covered in spines.

➤ A single female crown-of-thorns starfish can lay up to 100 million eggs a year!

➤ It eats by turning its stomach inside out on the coral, **digesting** it, and slurping everything back inside.

—Dr. Helen Fox, Marine Conservation Biologist, World Wildlife Fund

13

Soon, there was white coral as far as the eye could see.

"I think this is the place," said Riley.

"I think you're right," said Wyland.

Coral Bleaching

➤ If climate change isn't slowed, almost all of the coral of Australia's Great Barrier Reef will be gone by 2050.

➤ Pollution, disease, and changes in salt levels and light can also cause coral bleaching.

➤ Before 1979, there were only three known coral bleaching events. There have been hundreds since then.

—Dr. Jennie Hoffman, Ph.D., Climate Adaptation Specialist—Marine, World Wildlife Fund

When they dove back into the water, they saw hundreds of crown-of-thorns starfish. The water looked especially **murky**, so they took water samples as well as placing more sensors. *Even in Australia, the water isn't always clean,* thought Riley. Wyland spotted a giant shell resting on the reef and took a picture of it.

Back on the ship, Wyland explained, "That shelled creature was a triton. Tritons are one of the only natural **predators** of crown-of-thorns starfish."

"The starfish that eat the coral," said Riley.

"That's right," said Wyland. "The tritons here need all the help they can get, since it looks like they are losing the battle. The reef is in a constant tug-of-war, and too many of one species can unbalance the ecosystem and threaten the reef."

Triton

➤ It is one of the world's largest marine snails. It grows up to 20 in. (50.8 cm) long.

➤ It grips its prey with its muscular foot and uses its toothy **radula** to saw through the tough skin of starfish.

➤ The triton's saliva paralyzes its prey.

—Stuart Campbell, Ph.D.,
Field Conservationist,
Wildlife Conservation
Society

That night, Uncle Max checked the sensor data on his laptop. "The good news is that all of the water sensors are working. The bad news is that the water here is 5.4 degrees Fahrenheit warmer than normal. It takes only a 3.6-degree rise to kill coral. There is only one more area of the reef to study on this trip, but it will take us all night to get there. It's a newly bleached area reported by **BleachWatch**."

BLEACHING

TEMPERATURE

AVERAGE

TIME

As Riley drifted off to sleep, the whirring of the boat's motor reminded him of his mom's vacuum cleaner. He dreamed of giant tritons vacuuming up all the crown-of-thorns starfish.

Lionfish

➤ It gets its name from its large dorsal (back) fin and pectoral (side) fins, which form what looks like a lion's mane.

➤ The lionfish traps its prey with its pectoral fins, stuns it with venom, then eats it in one gulp!

➤ It hunts shrimp, crab, or even other fish.

—Dr. Lynne R. Parenti, Curator of Fishes and Research Scientist, National Museum of Natural History, Smithsonian Institution

The next day, Aunt Martha and Wyland swam out to take photos of the newly bleached coral. Some areas looked perfectly healthy, while others were white as snow. Uncle Max, Riley, and Alice got into an old dinghy to collect some surface water samples. They motored around a small island and into the open ocean.

"There's a dugong," said Uncle Max. "Dugongs are endangered marine mammals related to manatees and elephants. Rising ocean temperatures are destroying the beds of sea grass that are their main food source."

Dugong

➤ The endangered dugong can live up to 70 years, grow up to 10 ft. (3.05 m) long, and weigh as much as 1,000 lb. (454 kg).

➤ It is the only **herbivorous** sea mammal and is nicknamed the "sea cow."

➤ It floats so well that it has very thick, heavy bones to help it swim underwater.

—Alfonso Lombana, Marine Conservation Biologist, World Wildlife Fund

The dugong seemed to be playing a slow and graceful game of hide-and-seek, when suddenly it dove under and fled.

"SHARK!" yelled Uncle Max, revving the engine to get away. Alice and Riley quickly pulled their samples in.

"That poor dugong!" said Alice.

"Both species need to eat. The shark's survival depends on catching a dugong once in a while," said Uncle Max. "It's unusual to see a great white this far north, but not unheard of."

A black boat sped into view, just missing the shark. The surprised shark quickly turned around and swam back into the deep blue sea.

Great White Shark

➤ It has many rows of teeth. If any front teeth break off while the shark is hunting, they are quickly replaced by teeth from the back rows.

➤ It gets its name from the white color of its belly.

➤ It is the largest **predatory** shark, reaching up to 22.3 ft. (6.8 m) in length.

—Victor G. Springer,
Senior Scientist
Emeritus, Division of
Fishes, National Museum
of Natural History,
Smithsonian Institution

Suddenly, the overworked
engine sputtered and went silent.
"I think this dinghy has seen
better days," said Uncle Max as
he tinkered with the motor. Alice
tried to call Aunt Martha and
Wyland.

"The radio isn't working,
either," said Alice.

24

"The island is probably blocking our signal," said Uncle Max.

"I bet the black boat could help us!" cried Riley.

Uncle Max and Alice shouted and waved.

"Oh no!" said Riley, peering through the **binoculars**. "Those are poachers, and they're stealing tritons!"

25

"What now?" cried Alice. "Without power, we'll just drift out to sea. The sharks will love that!"

"I think I can tow us back," said Riley.

"Are you crazy?" asked Alice. "It's way too far to swim. Besides, how can you tow a boat?"

"Easy," said Riley, reaching into his backpack. "I'll use my personal scuba scooter. Wyland loaned it to me this morning."

"Brilliant!" said Uncle Max. "I'll attach a rope to the dinghy and you can pull us back."

27

Riley's idea worked perfectly.

Coral
➤ A coral colony can be as big as a school bus or as small as a grain of rice. Both sizes exist on the Great Barrier Reef.

➤ There are about 800 species of stony corals, half of which live on the Great Barrier Reef.

➤ A coral can live to be a thousand years old!

—Stephen D. Cairns,
Research Scientist,
Smithsonian Institution

"I see our boat!" cried Alice.

Uncle Max tried the radio one more time.

"Martha, Wyland, come in," said Uncle Max.

"What's wrong?" said Aunt Martha. "And where's Riley?"

"He's our tow truck," said Uncle Max. "I'll explain later. Right now, I need you to call the police. We saw some triton poachers on the other side of the island."

In a matter of minutes, a police helicopter was circling nearby.

"Riley, you and Alice were amazing," said Wyland. "You helped us catch triton poachers and showed that water temperatures are rising around the reef. Plus, the water samples you collected showed large amounts of **sediment** and pollution in the water. These all lead to coral bleaching, a problem that is getting worse every year."

"What can we do?" asked Riley.

30

"We need to take better care of the world's water," said Wyland. "Water covers almost 80 percent of the earth and helps connect us together as a planet, yet human-made climate change and pollution are creating oceans that aren't healthy for coral. What you do at your house halfway around the world affects the reef and the balance of nature. Using less energy can help slow down climate change. Conserving water and keeping it clean will help make sure that people and coral everywhere have enough cool, pure water to grow and be healthy."

"Clean water would definitely paint a brighter future for coral reefs!" said Riley.

31

Back home, Riley shared what he learned about the importance of clean water. He helped his father replace old faucets and showerheads with energy-saving filters that **purify** and reduce the amount of water they use. He told his family the story of the living reef, the great white shark, and meeting Wyland. He returned to living the life of a nine-year-old, until he once again heard from Uncle Max.

Where will Riley go next?

Further Information

Glossary

algae: plantlike creatures that live in the water and range in size from a single cell to large seaweeds

binoculars: handheld glasses with several lenses that can focus on faraway objects and make them appear much closer

BleachWatch: a program in which the public works with reef managers to spot signs of coral bleaching along a reef

digesting: breaking down food into nutrients that are absorbed by the body

herbivorous: eats only plants

larva: the early form of an animal that will change shape at adulthood

murky: dark and dirty

polyp: a coral, attached to a reef, that has a column-shaped body and an opening with a mouth and tentacles

predators: animals that consume (eat) other living things

purify: make clean

radula: a tonguelike part of a mollusk that's covered in small teeth and used to scrape food from surfaces and put it into the mouth

sediment: small, grainy matter, such as dirt or sand, that is moved and deposited by wind, water, or ice

tentacles: long, skinny, flexible arms used for touching, grabbing, or moving

Great Barrier Reef

Queensland

New Guinea

INDIAN OCEAN

Northern Territory

Western Australia

South Australia

Queensland

Brisbane

New South Wales

Victoria

INDIAN OCEAN

Tasmania

TASMAN SEA

New Zealand

CORAL SEA

PACIFIC OCEAN

Australia

N W E S

Wyland and Water

Wyland is a world-famous marine life artist and an activist for marine resource and water conservation. In addition, he is a gifted sculptor, photographer, writer, and scuba diver. His giant marine-life murals (he painted 100 by 2008) span 12 countries and four continents. For more than 25 years, Wyland has traveled the world, capturing the power and beauty of the undersea universe with his art while inspiring and educating others to conserve and preserve our planet and its precious resources.

Coral

Careful! Coral is alive and part of the reef. Touching or stepping on it can damage or even kill it. Without coral, fish have no reason to stay, and we would have nothing left to see.

JOIN US FOR MORE GREAT ADVENTURES!

RILEY'S WORLD™

Visit our Web site at

www.adventuresofriley.com

to find out how
you can join Riley's
super kids' club!

ADVENTURES OF RILEY®

Look for these other great Riley books:

- ➤ Safari in South Africa
- ➤ Project Panda
- ➤ South Pole Penguins
- ➤ Polar Bear Puzzle
- ➤ Dolphins in Danger
- ➤ Tigers in Terai